ACKNOWLEDGEMENTS

I would like to thank the following individuals for all their efforts in this book project:

Gordon McClelland for introducing me to Kerne Erickson. Kerne Erickson for his tireless efforts in creating the Banana Baby imagery. Joan Corman for assisting Kerne Erickson. Reina Herrera for her assistance in completing this project and for always being there to assist in anyway. Art Fisher for making this project and all projects come to life. Bernard Fickert and all the employees at Pacifica Island Art, Inc. for their continued support throughout the years.

I would also like to thank my son Jozef for always being a wonderful and loving son and my daughter Mia for being a beautiful and loving daughter. Thank you Mia for inspiring me to create Banana Baby.

I want to thank my close friend Judi Mjelde for her major contributions to this story. I am grateful to have such a wonderful friend as Judi. She is an inspiration to me and others, thank you Judi!

Greg Young
President
Greg Young Publishing, Inc.

GREG YOUNG PUBLISHING, INC.
P.O. BOX 2487
SANTA BARBARA, CALIFORNIA 93120
www.gregyoungpublishing.com
www.kerneerickson.com
e-mail: sales@gregyoungpublishing.com

ISBN: 978-1-933735-57-3
Printed in China

Library of Congress Control Number: 2009938361

PUBLISHED BY PACIFICA ISLAND ART, INC.
P.O. BOX 120
HAIKU, HAWAII 96708

800-222-7327 (US and Canada)
808-575-7696 (International and Local)
www.islandartstore.com

bananababy.com

BANANA BABY IN WAIKIKI

by Judi Mjelde and Greg Young

Design & Illustrations by Kerne Erickson
with Joan Corman

The surf was big and the tide was high
as suds of waves came crashing by.

On the sand with a pale and shovel in hand
Banana Baby discovered a canoe
docked by a fruit stand.

She smiled as she climbed
into the canoe.

Banana Baby discovered a bright colored blanket that was yellow and blue.

She tossed the blanket over her body
and placed her seashells in her lap.

....and decided this was a wonderful time to take a nap.

The trade winds kicked up,
and the tide came in.
Soon the canoe began to spin.

The canoe was set free, and it drifted out to sea. Monk Seals began to squeal, and Banana Baby woke up suddenly.

She rubbed her eyes and was completely
surprised to see that she was
now on an adventure
in Waikiki.

There were surfers catching waves
and dolphins riding the tide.

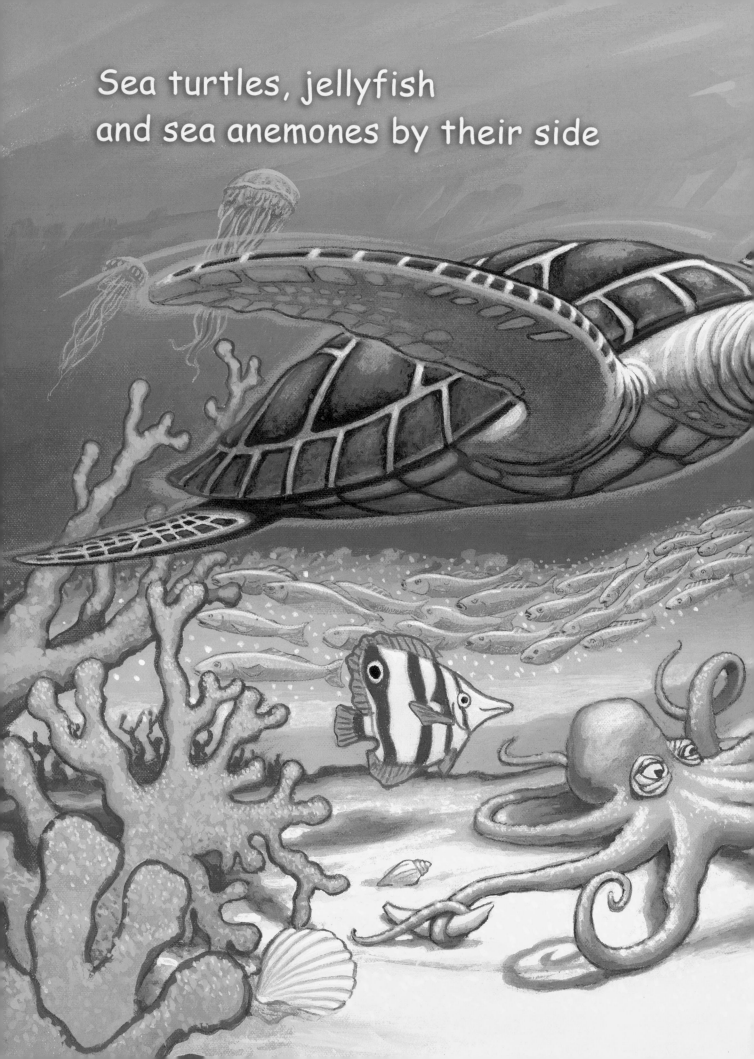

Sea turtles, jellyfish
and sea anemones by their side

Wrapped around the magnificent mountain known as Diamond Head a rainbow was in full sight.

Banana Baby was overwhelmed with a visual delight.

From a distance Banana Baby could see pineapple fields and banana trees. Looking at the banana trees made her hungry and......

.....she knew it was time to end her adventure at sea. She used her shovel as an ore and paddled back to the shore.

Banana Baby
enjoyed her voyage
at sea, but next time
she will take naps on
land in Waikiki.